AF427831

LILLY'S

RAGS TO RICHES

Lilly Lindsay

ISBN 979-8-89130-488-8 (paperback)
ISBN 979-8-89130-489-5 (digital)

Copyright © 2024 by Lilly Lindsay

All rights reserved. No part of this publication may be reproduced, distributed, or transmitted in any form or by any means, including photocopying, recording, or other electronic or mechanical methods without the prior written permission of the publisher. For permission requests, solicit the publisher via the address below.

Christian Faith Publishing
832 Park Avenue
Meadville, PA 16335
www.christianfaithpublishing.com

Printed in the United States of America

CONTENTS

What Is One of Your Favorite
Children's Stories? 1

What Was Your Mom Like
When You Were a Child?....................... 3

What Were Your Favorite Toys
as a Child? 5

What Are Some Choices You
Made About How to Raise Yourself?...... 7

What Were Your Grandparents Like?..... 9

What Was Your First Big Trip? 13

When Did You Get Your First Car?.......16

What Is Your Perfect Way of
Happiness? 19

Was There Anything Unusual
About Your Birth? 21

Acknowledgments 23

What Is One of Your Favorite Children's Stories?

I had several childhood stories growing up. *Sleeping Beauty*, *Snow White*, and *Cinderella*— out of the three, I would pick *Cinderella* as my favorite. Cinderella's story was a lot like mine in today's time. I married a man who was my prince in shining armor, who rescued me. We fell in love, and he married me and gave me a beautiful life with our six kids. He was kind and loving, a very good provider, and a very generous man. With his wealth, he gave me and his kids a life like the Brady Bunch, with maids and servants. With Emmett not being able to work, our funds got low and all the luxuries had to be taken away because of lack of funds. Even though Princess Lilly became the servant girl, and all their hired hands had been removed, I had to do all the housekeeping chores, like washing, cleaning, and scrubbing floors daily, even the yard work—getting dirt on my clothes from maintaining the yard reminds me of the Cinderella story before she turned into a beautiful princess.

What Was Your Mom Like When You Were a Child?

My mother was born in Aliceville, Alabama, a dark-skinned woman, short in height at five feet and six and a half inches. Her weight must have been around a hundred and forty pounds or so at that time. She had a beautiful smooth complexion with dark, thick, shoulder-length hair. She was a hard worker too. Although she never had much of an education in her day, she was a bright young girl. Her family was poor and uneducated, and they did not know how to give her a structured life. Mattie needed to help with family expenses, so at twelve years old, Mattie worked from sunup to sundown in a cotton field with her sister, Minnie. This lasted every day until she was about sixteen and left Aliceville, Alabama, heading north to Detroit, Michigan. There she married at the age of twenty and had three beautiful girls, Laverne, Rosemary, and Lilly. She and Austin attended church on Sundays with the girls. He worked for Chrysler, where he designed car engines. Mattie loved canning, gardening, sewing, quilting, fishing, and cooking her collard greens with freshwater fish. She departed this life at the age of eighty years old.

What Were Your Favorite Toys as a Child?

Dolls of all kinds—from ceramic and paper to plastic—were my companions. My favorite dolls were the plastic and paper ones, especially the Barbie and Ken dolls, which I loved. I would spend most of my time daydreaming about being just like Barbie, as pretty as she looked and dressed. My paper dolls were my own creations: I would draw and color them in all shades, and sometimes I'd even make pendants with ceramic bodies. I was always an arts and crafts person, even as a child. I fantasized about being a princess trapped in a tower, hoping Ken would come to rescue me. And you know what? He did. One sunny day, as I stood by my tower window feeding birds, I heard the sounds of galloping horses. As the noise subsided, I looked down to see a tall, well-dressed man on a white horse. A voice called out, "What a beautiful day this is!" As he introduced himself, he told me his name was Ken and explained he was in the area for bird hunting. I introduced myself as Barbie. He then asked if I would like to have a cup of tea over a picnic, and I said I would be more than happy to. From that day on, we stayed together forever, and he became my true love, and we lived happily ever after.

What Are Some Choices You Made About How to Raise Yourself?

First, let me introduce myself: My name is Lilly. The choices I would make about how I would raise myself better would be as follows. The foremost priority for me is never wanting to be overweight or unhealthy. I would maintain my body weight at around 120 pounds, appropriate for a woman who is five feet and four inches tall. I'd prefer a clean scent, perhaps a sweet perfume, and well-shampooed hair. I would take hot showers or baths daily. Completing school and college is also important to me, enabling a better career choice for self-support. Later on, I'd travel the world, get married, have children, and maintain regular church attendance. I'd have a good social lifestyle with educated individuals like myself, exercise regularly, enjoy a good book, watch soft jazz music movies on TV for relaxation, and relish romantic dinner outings with close friends and family. I'd prioritize a stress-free life, sanity, and good memory. Did I mention the importance of maintaining a decent body? I'd aim to stay as healthy as possible to enjoy a long, beautiful life with my family and kids. Those are just a few things on how I would raise myself better. Lastly, I'd take a European cruise on the Viking cruise ship with my children for company. That defines happiness for me. Also, making better choices, maintaining a positive mind, and keeping negativity at bay is essential.

What Were Your Grandparents Like?

Well, I only knew my mother's mother from her side of the family. I never knew my granddad personally. However, I heard great and fascinating stories about his life. He was a poor, uneducated man who had roughly a sixth-grade education. He worked hard and helped his parents raise his sister and brothers. Eventually, he grew up and met my grandmother, my Nana, Annie Pearl Wilkens, who was born in the South, in Aliceville, Alabama. Interestingly, they say this place can't even be found on a map. They worked in a cotton field together; that's how they met. They worked there alongside other slaves. The two of them became very close friends, fell in love, and got married. He was a good and loving husband to my Nana. Two years after their wedding, they began their family and had two beautiful girls, Minnie and Mattie. Sadly, he fell ill and passed away. In those times, people of color and Whites could not be together; the consequences were dire, sometimes even lynching.

Now my grandmother Annie was a very strict woman who believed in hard work and discipline. There was no such thing with my grandmother as *couch potatoes*. Watching TV and lazily flipping channels? That was a no-no. You did chores, took your bath, and got ready for the next day. If you were lucky, you got supper. Every night, my Nana read a Bible scripture to them: "Our Father which art in heaven, keep us safe, Lord, from hanging." That's how the story was relayed to us. The only book she'd allow anyone to read was the Bible, at least for those who could read. They didn't have a TV, but they made their own music, singing as they picked cotton. They did, however, have a small radio to check the weather and music and, when she moved up north, listen to some tunes.

Every morning, she'd rise with the roosters and start her day—collecting eggs in the chicken house, cleaning stalls for the horses, feeding pigs, and milking cows. In Alabama, she also worked on a plantation. Her duties included indoor chores like cooking, cleaning, scrubbing floors, and making beds. When outside, she worked in the cotton fields, filling bags with the cotton that she had picked for that day. She often talked about how tiring it was, especially scrubbing floors until her knees became raw. After a long day of work, she faced a two- to three-mile walk to catch a bus ride home.

She was a woman who loved God and her children dearly. She moved to Michigan when her daughter Mattie was about to give birth to Lavern, born on December 12, 1953. That's how Nana Annie ended up in the northern state of Michigan. After a ten- to twelve-hour bus ride, she arrived in Detroit, Michigan, meeting Mattie at Grace Hospital with her first grandchild. Annie eventually settled on Brady Street in Detroit's east side, helping Mattie raise her granddaughter. Years passed, and Annie was diagnosed with cancer and was forced to retire because of illness. She retired from her job at Detroit Receiving Hospital as a lab tech. Born on June 15, 1906, she passed away in 2004.

What Was Your
First Big Trip?

My first big trip was to Hawaii for my wedding anniversary in September 1981. My husband, Emmett, and I sailed on the Royal Caribbean cruise ship to celebrate. It was a land-and-sea cruise, and we stayed in Hawaii for ten days. We visited several different places on the Big Island. For five days, we stayed off the ship on Lanai. Our first port was Kaul in Hawaii, known as the Garden Island. Personally, I wouldn't want to live there; they have too many birds for my liking. The second port was the Big

Island of Hawaii, where we stayed for two days. The last port was Lanai, the Pineapple Island.

The most beautiful spot during our trip was Hanauma Bay-Osha. Its scenery at sunset was mesmerizing, especially in 1981, at the time I was there. The weather was perfect, the water was crystal blue-green, and the food was delicious. The scenery was like a paradise, so beautiful it was beyond comparison. If I recall correctly, we stayed on the cruise for five days. Remembering the exact length is a little challenging for me, but I believe we spent five days at sea, traveling to and from the ports.

The boat ride was enjoyable. The water was not choppy, and the ship sailed so smoothly that it felt as if we were standing on land rather than water. It's hard to believe, but that's how smooth the journey was for us. Many people get seasick from choppy waters. Boy was God good to us on our trip. On my first cruise travel, I did not get seasick at all. Our trip was remarkably calm. Every day at sea was smooth, and I didn't experience seasickness.

While at sea, you can shop, dine, and enjoy onboard entertainment. After winding down, you can change into swimwear and relax by the pool with a night swim. It was delightful listening to bands play island music with a drink in hand, especially after a swim, as we journeyed to the next stop.

I plan to go back to Hawaii before I turn seventy-five, which will be in 2033. That was my first big trip, and it was a land-and-sea cruise. I must say, I preferred the cruise part of our journey. We enjoyed it so much that we decided to cruise every year for our anniversary. Now, in 2023, we've taken at least twenty cruises to celebrate. While I enjoy land travel, cruising is my top choice.

When Did You Get
Your First Car?

My first car was acquired in 1976, a gift from my stepdad, Lawrence Starks. As I recall, to the best of my knowledge, I must have been around twenty years old. My father, Lawrence Starks, had purchased a newer car that year, and instead of trading in his old one, he gave it to me. My first car was an old, rusted Ford. It was brown and had four doors, with a rusted-out floor on the passenger's side of the front seat that your feet could almost touch the ground from a large hole that was on the floor. It reminded me of the Flintstones' car—remember that classic cartoon where Fred had to run with his feet to drive? Passengers in my car had a similar experience, though they didn't exclaim "Yabba dabba doo!" when taking off as Fred did. When riding in my Ford, you had to hold your feet in your lap to ensure they didn't drag on the ground. I'll never forget that car. Recounting the memories of my old jalopy can induce fits of laughter.

Despite its appearance, I was thrilled to have it. No longer did I have to wait in the cold for the bus, sometimes standing for over an hour in snowy, frigid weather. That car saved me from having frostbitten hands and face, providing a warm seat with heat and wheels. It was dependable as much as I needed it to be. It took me safely everywhere I needed to go. I no longer had to ride the bus back and forth to work. I was grateful for the ability to drive instead of relying on public transportation. It safely transported me throughout the city whenever I needed it.

What Is Your Perfect Way of Happiness?

Peace of mind! For me, nothing is better than peace of mind in a calm, quiet, and stress-free environment. Not having a care in the world, just laid-back and cruising around the Mediterranean Sea. Let's travel to Europe and take an all-inclusive European cruise on the Viking cruise ship. After checking in on board and changing into something more comfortable, I head to the deck. I'm thrilled to be on the Viking, noted as the number 1 cruise ship for European travels. As I navigate among the passengers, I search for a seat by the pool to "let my hair down," as we girls say. The view is breathtaking; the water's greenish-blue hue is mesmerizing. Sitting with a book by the pool, sipping on a cold beverage, and enjoying the music—it's finally quality time for me. I'm eagerly awaiting the moment I step foot on land in my first European port, ready for shopping. Oh, and did I mention I'm quite the shopaholic? That, for me, is true happiness. I truly need that vacation time.

Was There Anything Unusual About Your Birth?

Yes, there was: I am a leap-year baby, born on September 28, 1956. A leap year is a calendar year that contains an additional day added to keep the calendar year synchronized with the astronomical or seasonal year. For example, the date spans from Monday, January 1, 2024, to Tuesday, December 31, 2024. In my research on leap-year babies, I found that there are four million people in the world who are leap-day babies. Such individuals are called *leapers* or *leaplings*.

Acknowledgments

I want to give thanks to God, who is the head of my life; second, to my husband, Emmett, and my three sons; third, and most importantly, to Brandon, my youngest son, who encourages me, and to everyone for all their support.

Thank you.

About the Author

Her life was amazing. She was always authentically herself and very accessible. Her skills are limitless. She ages like a fine wine and is also a role model for women's fashion. Growing older and wiser every day, she is honest, dependable, and one of the best people you could have as a friend on God's green earth. A strong woman in faith who loves God, she is passionate about music, dance, and the arts. Married with children, she enjoys tennis and golf and is a skilled cook. She always lends a helping hand to those in need.

www.ingramcontent.com/pod-product-compliance
Lightning Source LLC
Chambersburg PA
CBHW020656160726
47991CB00003B/1218